DreamWorks & Aardman
Flushed Away™

MOVIE STORYBOOK

Adapted by Sarah Durkee
Pencils by Mike Morris   Color by Barry Gott

SCHOLASTIC

Roderick St. James of Kensington lived in London. And when his owner, Tabitha, left town, he had the apartment all to himself. The fancy cage. The gourmet food. The sports car. Even the companionship of glamorous plastic fashion dolls! Who cared that they couldn't talk? Roddy thought he had everything a pet rat could ever want.

One night, a strange gurgling sound came from the kitchen. It was Sid, a glop-covered sewer rat who'd come up through the drain. He liked Roddy's home a lot, and wanted to stay. Roddy was horrified. He'd never known rats could be so filthy, so disgusting, so . . . *ratty*!

Roddy had a plan to get rid of Sid fast.

"Perhaps sir would like to take a spin in the whirlpool?" he asked.

Sid wasn't THAT dumb. He knew a toilet when he saw one. He pushed Roddy in instead.

"Bon voyage!" he cackled, flushing Roddy down to a watery fate.

Roddy blasted down through the pipes, finally splashing into . . .
"The sewer??" he cried. Roddy panicked. All around him was
a maze of dark and dripping tunnels, and he was very alone.
Except for hundreds of slugs.

"AAAAAAARGH!!!!" Roddy screamed.

"AAAAAAARGH!!!!" the terrified slugs screamed back.

Then, pushing through a metal hatch, Roddy discovered a bustling, underground city of rats!

All Roddy wanted to do was get back home. He found his way to a boat called the *Jammy Dodger* and asked Rita, the captain, for help.

"I've got my own problems, mate," said Rita, unimpressed with this prissy-looking trespasser. Suddenly, their conversation was interrupted by the arrival of two more rats: the very nasty Spike and the very large Whitey.

"**W**here's the ruby, Rita?" Spike demanded.

"The boss wants it back," growled Whitey.

"I don't have your stupid ruby!" Rita insisted.

More hench-rats came aboard and searched the *Jammy Dodger*. Roddy really wanted to get out of this mess. Suddenly he noticed an odd shape to Rita's trousers, and pointed it out.

"You little snitch!" Rita cried.

"The booty's in the booty!" Whitey said triumphantly, shaking Rita upside down until a huge ruby fell out.

Spike and Whitey took their captives to the hideaway of their evil, scheming boss, The Toad. Roddy took credit for finding the ruby and asked The Toad to help him get back home. The Toad was impressed with his posh guest and decided to show Roddy his collection of royal souvenirs.

"Amusing!" proclaimed Roddy. That was a *big* mistake. The Toad took his tacky collection very seriously.

"Amusing??" The Toad roared, as his chin blew up so much it practically exploded. "Ice them both!" he ordered.

Imprisoned in a huge freezer, surrounded by The Toad's frozen victims, Rita managed to pick the lock on their chains. As the freezer filled with nitrogen gas, Rita and Roddy made a quick exit, leaving Spike and Whitey behind in their very own ice cube for two.

"The prize returns to me, you big, fat, slimy airbag!" Rita crowed to The Toad, holding up the ruby as she planned her escape. But how? Rita yanked an electric cable out of its socket. She had an idea.

"Not the master cable!" howled The Toad as the power and the lights went out.

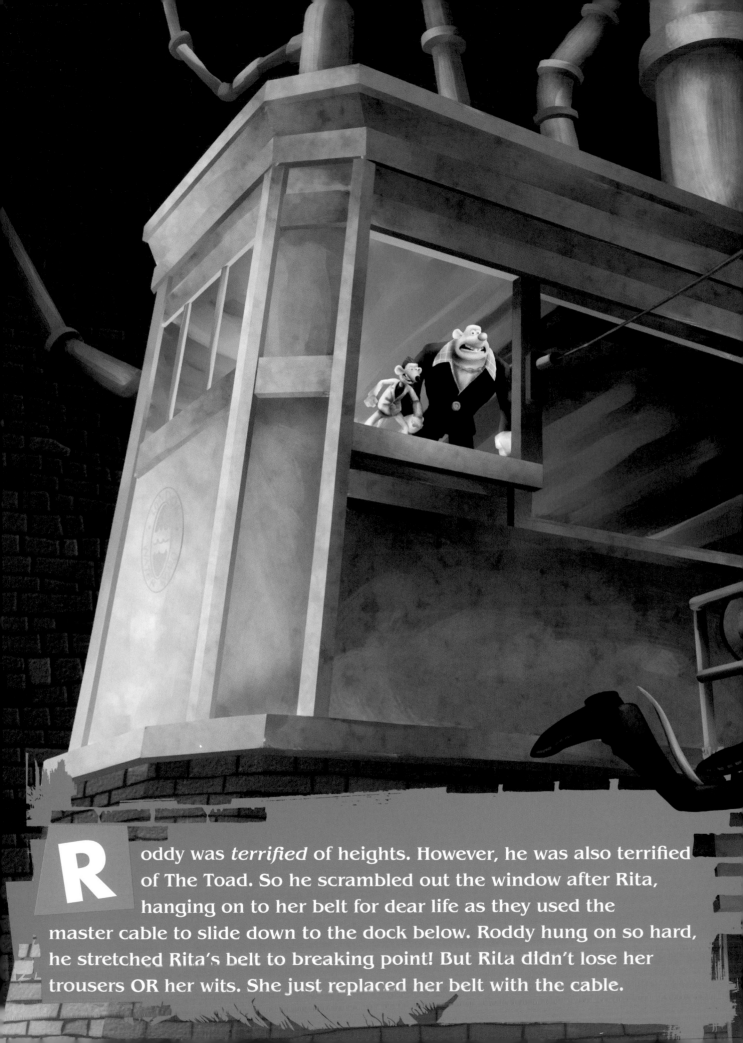

Roddy was *terrified* of heights. However, he was also terrified of The Toad. So he scrambled out the window after Rita, hanging on to her belt for dear life as they used the master cable to slide down to the dock below. Roddy hung on so hard, he stretched Rita's belt to breaking point! But Rita didn't lose her trousers OR her wits. She just replaced her belt with the cable.

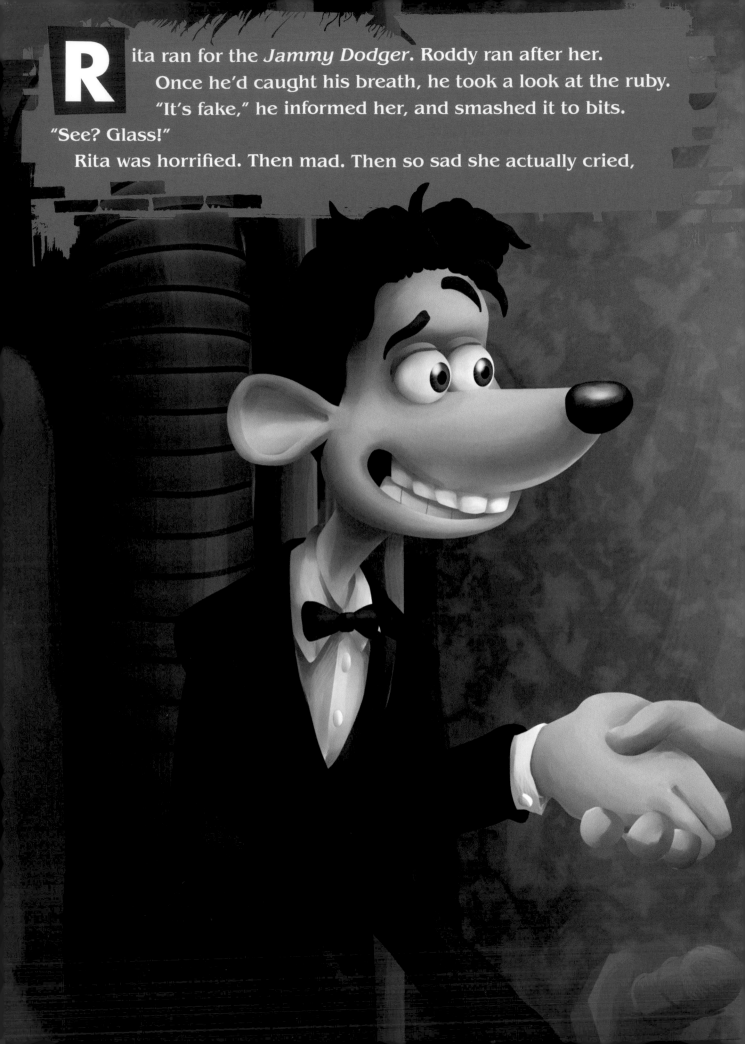

Rita ran for the *Jammy Dodger*. Roddy ran after her. Once he'd caught his breath, he took a look at the ruby. "It's fake," he informed her, and smashed it to bits. "See? Glass!"

Rita was horrified. Then mad. Then so sad she actually cried,

which a cool rat like Rita hardly ever did. When Roddy found out how much having a real ruby had meant to Rita and her family, he felt awful.

"If you get me back home, I'll make you rich beyond your wildest dreams!" he promised. Rita decided to trust him, and they sealed the deal with a handshake.

"**F**orget the ruby!" The Toad bellowed to Spike and Whitey when they brought back nothing but a handful of broken red glass. "It's the *master cable* I want! Without it, my plan is ruined!"

Spike and Whitey didn't understand, but then they often didn't.

"You need to be back in time for the World Cup Final!" The Toad screamed.

"Ooh, great, are we watching the game together, boss?" said Spike.

"No, we are not! Just get me the cable!"

Rita took Roddy to her family's house. He met her mother and father and most of her 36 sisters and brothers.

Rita told her dad about the plan to get Roddy home, and that he'd repay her with riches beyond their dreams. But Rita's dad was worried it was too dangerous.

Suddenly Liam held up a WANTED poster with Roddy's picture on it. "I've got a plan," he said.

Roddy overheard Rita talking with her dad and Liam about turning him in for the reward money. He couldn't believe she'd betray him.

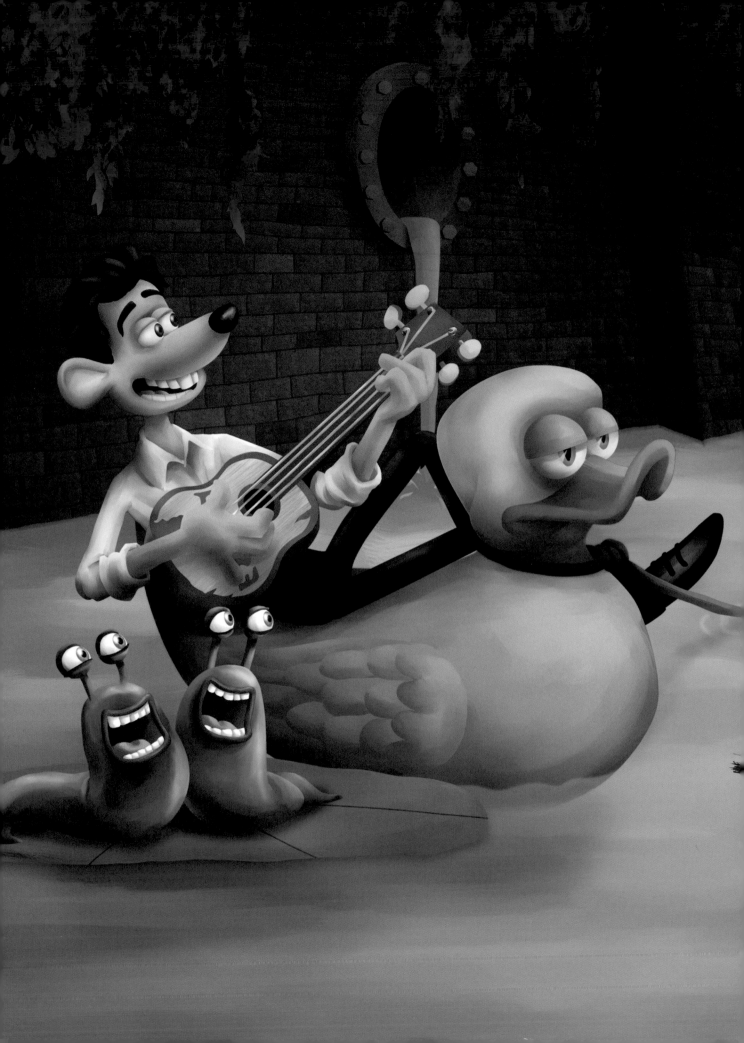

Roddy took off in the *Jammy Dodger* without Rita. When he ran out of gas, Rita caught up with him. Roddy confronted her.

"That was my stupid little brother's plan," she told him, "and no one listens to him."

To teach Roddy a lesson, Rita made him row a rubber duck with a ukulele.

"Ice-cold Ree-tah," he sang as he sailed behind the boat, "won't you be sweet-ah to meeee?"

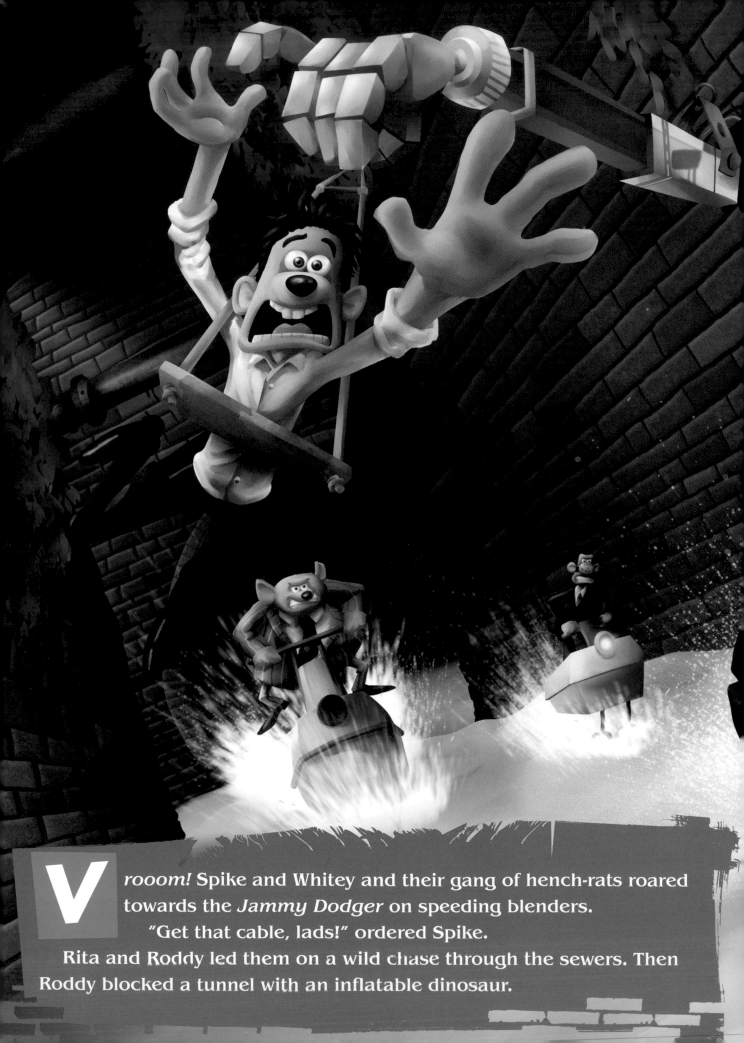

Vrooom! Spike and Whitey and their gang of hench-rats roared towards the *Jammy Dodger* on speeding blenders.

"Get that cable, lads!" ordered Spike.

Rita and Roddy led them on a wild chase through the sewers. Then Roddy blocked a tunnel with an inflatable dinosaur.

"We did it!" Roddy cheered. The dinosaur popped. "We didn't do it!" he corrected. Rita finally used her secret weapon: the Red Button. The *Jammy Dodger* raced away.

Spike and Whitey had a sinking feeling that this would be tough to explain to the boss.

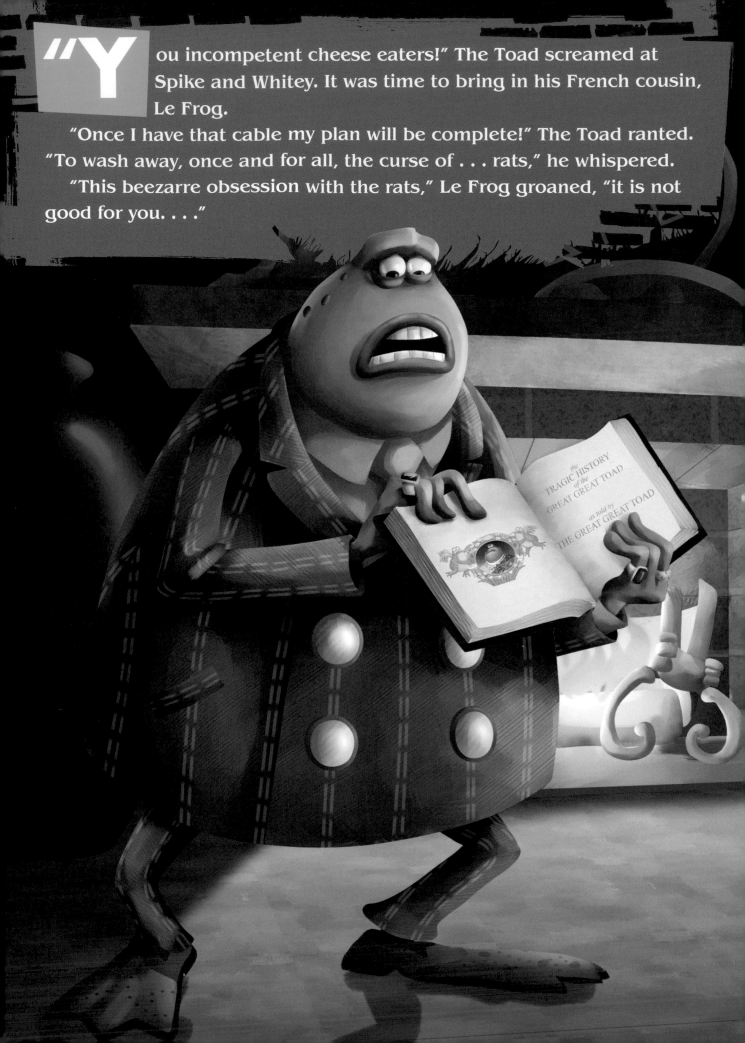

"**Y**ou incompetent cheese eaters!" The Toad screamed at Spike and Whitey. It was time to bring in his French cousin, Le Frog.

"Once I have that cable my plan will be complete!" The Toad ranted. "To wash away, once and for all, the curse of . . . rats," he whispered.

"This beezarre obsession with the rats," Le Frog groaned, "it is not good for you. . . ."

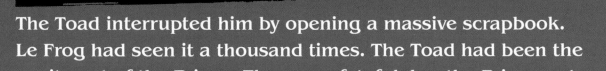

The Toad interrupted him by opening a massive scrapbook.

Le Frog had seen it a thousand times. The Toad had been the favourite pet of the Prince. Then, one fateful day, the Prince got a pet rat. And The Toad was flushed . . .

"Boo hoo hoo!" mocked Le Frog.

"JUST GET THE CABLE!" roared The Toad.

Le Frog snapped his fingers, and his team of trained hench-frogs jumped to the ready.

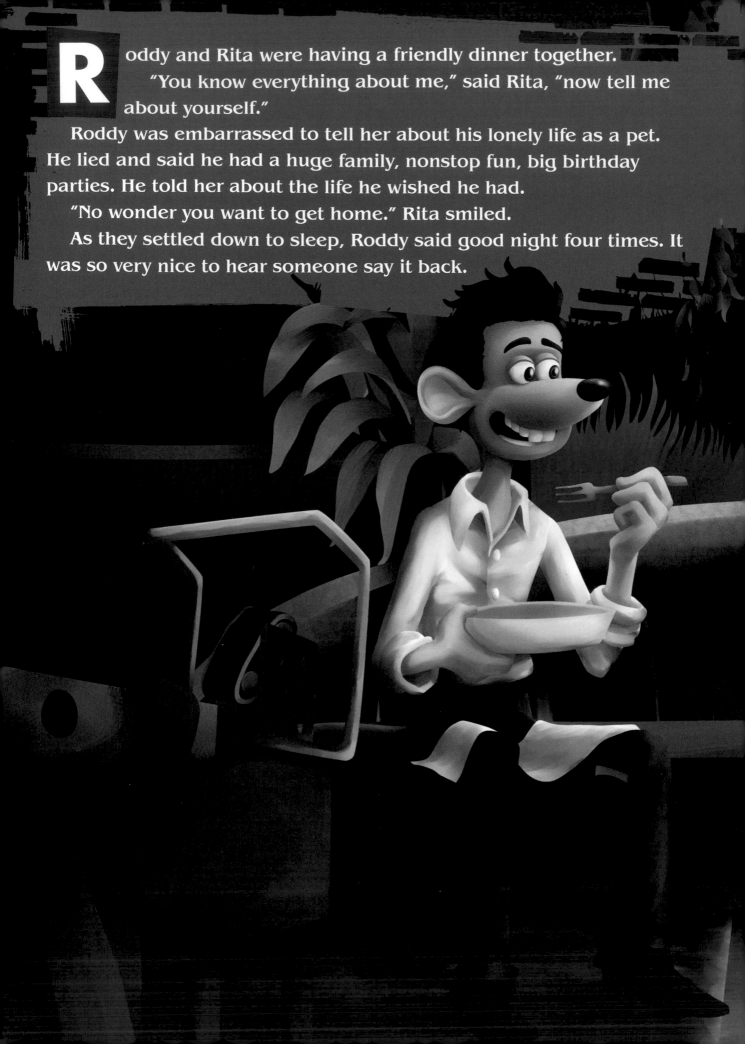

Roddy and Rita were having a friendly dinner together.

"You know everything about me," said Rita, "now tell me about yourself."

Roddy was embarrassed to tell her about his lonely life as a pet. He lied and said he had a huge family, nonstop fun, big birthday parties. He told her about the life he wished he had.

"No wonder you want to get home." Rita smiled.

As they settled down to sleep, Roddy said good night four times. It was so very nice to hear someone say it back.

The next morning, Roddy and Rita began the trip to Kensington. As the *Dodger* headed towards the rapids, Le Frog and his hench-frogs attacked! Marcel, a mime frog, wore a video phone showing The Toad's furious face.

"Get that cable!" The Toad commanded.

The *Jammy Dodger* began to drop over the waterfall, but the grabber arm held on to an overhead pipe! Rita clung to the boat with one hand and Roddy with the other. Le Frog slimed his way towards Rita and pulled off her cable belt.

"*Au revoir, ma chéri!*" he yelled, as the *Jammy Dodger* began to fall.

In the nick of time, Roddy and Rita turned a plastic bag into a parachute. As they floated past, Rita snatched the belt from Le Frog.

Up they rose, faster and faster, through a tall pipe and towards the light.

The sky over Kensington was beautiful and sunny. Roddy and Rita steered their parachute to Roddy's roof, let go, and plunged down the chimney, straight onto the soft white carpet. Home at last!

Roddy gave Rita the ruby he'd promised her, as well as another. Rita hugged Roddy gratefully. "I'd love to meet your family," she said. But there was no one to see . . . except for Sid. And Rita already knew Sid from the sewer.

When she saw Roddy's cage, she finally understood. "You're a pet, aren't you?" she asked.

Roddy was desperate to deny it and keep Rita's respect. "It's a palace," he bragged. But the words sounded hollow – even to him.

"Good-bye then, Roddy St. James. of Kensington," Rita said. And she walked away. A moment later, Roddy heard a flushing sound.

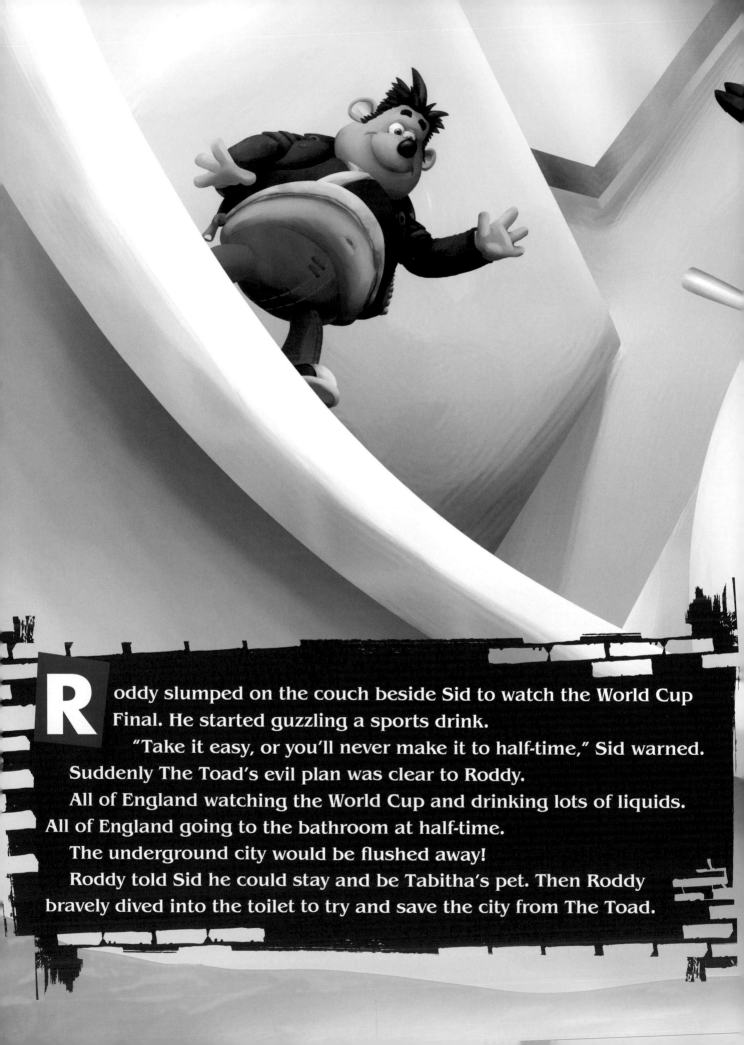

Roddy slumped on the couch beside Sid to watch the World Cup Final. He started guzzling a sports drink.

"Take it easy, or you'll never make it to half-time," Sid warned.

Suddenly The Toad's evil plan was clear to Roddy.

All of England watching the World Cup and drinking lots of liquids. All of England going to the bathroom at half-time.

The underground city would be flushed away!

Roddy told Sid he could stay and be Tabitha's pet. Then Roddy bravely dived into the toilet to try and save the city from The Toad.

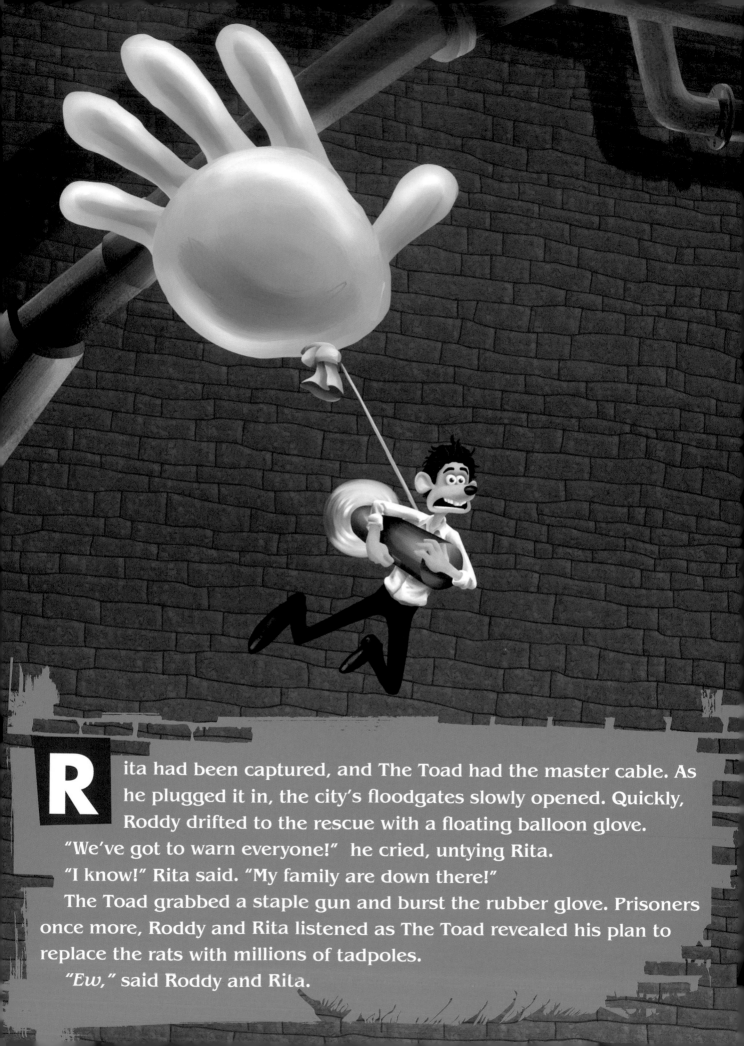

Rita had been captured, and The Toad had the master cable. As he plugged it in, the city's floodgates slowly opened. Quickly, Roddy drifted to the rescue with a floating balloon glove.

"We've got to warn everyone!" he cried, untying Rita.

"I know!" Rita said. "My family are down there!"

The Toad grabbed a staple gun and burst the rubber glove. Prisoners once more, Roddy and Rita listened as The Toad revealed his plan to replace the rats with millions of tadpoles.

"*Ew,*" said Roddy and Rita.

Roddy and Rita had to think fast. Roddy tugged at a pipe and liquid nitrogen poured out, freezing everything and everyone in its path . . . everyone except The Toad.

The half-time whistle blew! The Big Flush was coming!

"You and your kind are finished!" The Toad snarled. As he stepped forward, his foot froze to a leaky pipe. Suddenly Roddy knew what he had to do. He tricked The Toad into shooting out his tongue and it stuck in the floodgate gears. Then he froze Le Frog's foot to a pipe hanging in front of the floodgates. A huge wave thundered towards the crowd below, and it broke the nitrogen pipe! The rushing water froze into a giant wave of solid ice!

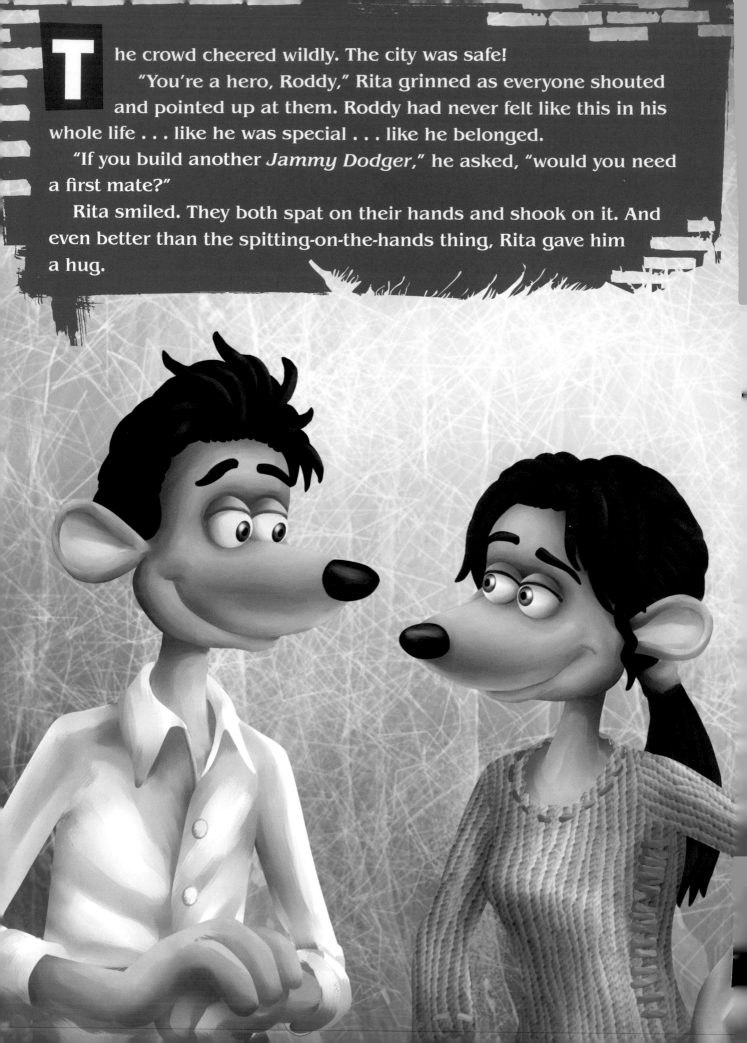

The crowd cheered wildly. The city was safe!

"You're a hero, Roddy," Rita grinned as everyone shouted and pointed up at them. Roddy had never felt like this in his whole life . . . like he was special . . . like he belonged.

"If you build another *Jammy Dodger*," he asked, "would you need a first mate?"

Rita smiled. They both spat on their hands and shook on it. And even better than the spitting-on-the-hands thing, Rita gave him a hug.

Scholastic Children's Books, Euston House,
24 Eversholt Street, London, NW1 1DB, UK
A division of Scholastic Ltd.

First published in the USA by Scholastic Inc., 2006
This edition first published in the UK by Scholastic Ltd, 2006

10 digit ISBN: 0 439 94368 X
13 digit ISBN: 978 0439 94368 0

Flushed Away © 2006 DreamWorks Animation L.L.C.
and Aardman Animations Ltd
Flushed Away™ Dreamworks Animation L.L.C

Printed and bound by Tien Wah Press Pte, Ltd, Malaysia
1 2 3 4 5 6 7 8 9 10